I KNEW TWO
WHO SAID MOO

I KNEW TWO WHO SAID MOO

a counting and rhyming book

written by
Judi Barrett

illustrated by
Daniel Moreton

atheneum books for young readers
New York   London   Toronto   Sydney   Singapore

Atheneum Books for Young Readers
An imprint of Simon & Schuster Children's Publishing Division
1230 Avenue of the Americas
New York, New York 10020

Book design by Daniel Moreton and Ann Bobco
The text of this book is set in Helvetica Rounded.
The illustrations are rendered in Adobe Illustrator.
Printed in Hong Kong

2 4 6 8 10 9 7 5 3 1
Library of Congress Cataloging-in-Publication Data
Barrett, Judi.
I knew two who said moo : a counting and rhyming
book / written by Judi Barrett ; illustrated by Daniel Moreton.
p. cm.
Summary: Rhyming lines feature the numbers from one to ten.
ISBN 0-689-82104-2 (alk. paper)
1. Counting—Juvenile literature. 2. English language—Rhyme
—Juvenile literature. [1. Counting. 2. English language—Rhyme.]
I. Moreton, Daniel, ill. II. Title.
QA113.B374 2000
513.2'11—dc21   99-31892

FIRST
EDITION

For one very special mom . . . mine. —j.b.

For my grandmother, whom I could always count on. —d.m.

I FOUND ONLY ONE
WEIGHING A TON
WHO HAD JUST BEGUN
LYING IN THE SUN
ON A TOASTED BUN
HAVING LOTS OF FUN
PLAYING THE ACCORDION
AND THINKING HE SHOULD RUN
BEFORE HE'S TOO WELL-DONE.

2

I KNEW TWO
WHO SAID MOO
ALL DRESSED IN BLUE
SITTING IN A SHOE
ON THE AVENUE
WITH NOSES THEY BLEW
BECAUSE OF THE FLU
GETTING A SHAMPOO
BEFORE THE BARBECUE
GIVEN BY THE KANGAROO
AND THE EWE
AT THE ZOO.
WHEW!

3

LISTEN TO ME.
AS YOU CAN SEE
THERE ARE JUST THREE
SITTING IN A TREE
ALL DRINKING TEA
AND EATING MACARONI
WHILE PLAYING A SYMPHONY.
ONE'S HOLDING A KEY.
ONE'S BALANCING A PEA
AND ONE HAS A BUMBLEBEE
ON ITS KNEE.
WE AGREE?

I MET FOUR
AT THE DOOR
WHEN IT STARTED TO POUR.
THEIR TOES WERE QUITE SORE
WHICH MADE THEM ALL ROAR
AND LIE DOWN ON THE FLOOR
AND WHAT'S MORE
THEY STARTED TO SNORE.

I WATCHED FIVE ARRIVE
AND SAW THEM DIVE
OFF THEIR HIVE
ONTO THE DRIVE.
THEY'RE ALL STILL ALIVE
AND I KNOW THEY'LL SURVIVE
AND MOST CERTAINLY THRIVE.

I NOTICED SIX
ALL HOLDING PICKS
TRYING TO MIX
A PILE OF BRICKS
WITH A BUNCH OF STICKS
SO THEY COULD FIX
THE HOUSE FOR THE CHICKS
WHO PERFORMED TRICKS
AND RECITED LIMERICKS.

I COUNTED JUST SEVEN
NOT ELEVEN
ALL JUMPING UP TOWARD HEAVEN
ONE'S NAME IS EVA
THREE ARE NAMED KEV
AND THREE ARE NAMED DEV
"EIGHTEEN," SHOUTED E
"IS ELEVEN PLUS SE

I HEARD THAT ALL EIGHT
ARRIVED LATE
AND WERE TOLD TO WAIT
AT THE GATE.
EACH BROUGHT A PLATE
BUT BEFORE THEY ATE
THEY WANTED TO STATE
"THIS FOOD IS GREAT!"
"IT'S BEANS WE HATE."

I NOTICED NINE
LOOKING JUST FINE
STANDING IN LINE
IN THE SUNSHINE
HOLDING BALLS OF TWINE
POINTING TO A PORCUPINE
WITH A VALENTINE
AND A BIG SIGN
SAYING "BE MINE."

ICE CR
99¢

CHOCOLATE
VANILLA
STRAWBERRY
DIRT
SLOP POPS
MUDDY BUDDIES
HEAVENLY HOG
SWINE SWIRL
ROCKY RUNT

THEN
I SAW TEN
WATCHING A HEN
NAMED GWEN
WRITING THE LETTER "N"
OVER AND OVER AGAIN
WITH A PEN
BORROWED FROM A WREN
NAMED BEN.